For my husband Kalle and my daughter Kwezi.
And for my grandmother Anna, who inspired me in so many ways
and told me these stories.

Published in 2003 by University of Natal Press
Private Bag X01
Scottsville, 3209
South Africa
Email: books@nu.ac.za
Website: www.unpress.co.za

© 2003 Text: Gcina Mhlophe
© 2003 Illustrations: The Individual Artists

ISBN 1-86914-035-4

Editor: Elana Bregin
Layout and Design: Flying Ant Designs
Cover Illustration: Kalle Becker

Printed and bound by Interpak Books, Pietermaritzburg

Stories of
AFRICA

by

Gcina Mhlophe

UNIVERSITY OF NATAL PRESS
Pietermaritzburg

AUTHOR'S NOTE

My grandmother was the first person to tell me stories. She encouraged my imagination to run wild, and I really believed in those laughing crocodiles and flying tortoises that she told me about. I loved her tales about the scary *amaZimzim* – the man-eating ogres – and many more fantastic creatures. Because of the way my grandmother told those stories to me, I learnt at a very young age to love language and to understand its power. But sometimes, when I have to express myself in English, which is the language I now use most often, I find that some things are not possible to say. Then I get frustrated and catch myself wishing that everyone spoke my mother tongue. Yet that never stops me from continuing to tell the wonderful stories of my people and share their imaginative richness with others.

Most of the stories in this book are taken from well-known traditional tales that the people of Africa have been telling to each other since the world began. Some of these stories from my childhood recur in different versions in many other parts of the world. This is proof to me of the way in which humans have always tried to make sense of life's mysteries and used stories to explain them to each other.

Is there still room for these ancient stories in our lives today? I say 'Yes!' Because of the flexibility of this medium, one story can be interpreted in a variety of ways, making it possible for audiences of different ages and cultures to find what they need in it.

One of my favourite stories is about the woman who went down to the bottom of the sea to look for stories to bring back for the human world. I have told this tale to audiences in different countries all over the world, and so many times I have had the response: 'You know, that story has made me realise that to find the answers I am looking for in my life, I need to look deep inside myself. I must search the depths of the ocean that is my own heart and soul.' Now what does a storyteller say to that?

I love sharing my stories with others and I also enjoy writing them down in books. But my favourite way of relating them is the ancient way of my people – telling them face to face, in front of a live audience. Oh the thrill of seeing the faces reacting to what you are saying, of feeling the energy go from storyteller to audience and back again! I hope that this book will carry some of that thrill to you, the reader, and that you, too, will feel a story awaken inside you and find yourself wishing to tell it to others. Yes, you! Because every living being has a story to tell.

So let's keep passing on the magic!

Gcina Mhlophe

——X——

CONTENTS

MAZANENDABA

Illustrations by Jeannie Kinsler

A LONG TIME AGO, so long ago that it is not important to remember exactly when, people lived in small little villages all around the world. In one such village, there was a woman called Mazanendaba. She lived in a beautiful house by the sea with her husband and children.

Mazanendaba loved her family very much. She taught her children skills like cooking and fetching water, collecting firewood and weaving grass mats and baskets. But most of all, what they enjoyed was to go swimming. They would go down to the beach and splash about in the waves and have a good time chasing each other. Sometimes they would catch a fish or two for lunch before coming back home to be with their father.

The father's name was Zenzele, a tall, strong man who made sculptures. If he saw a bird that he liked, he would keep its image fresh in his mind and then carve it out of wood and put it in the house, where they could all admire it. He would see a Springbok or a Kudu drinking from a waterhole, then rush home and carve it out of stone. Zenzele loved his work. As the years went by, his many beautiful stone and wood carvings came to decorate the inside and the outside of the house.

For a while Mazanendaba was happy with things the way they were. But presently she realised that something was missing in their lives. You see, there were no stories at that time. People used to sit around the fire after supper, and watch the stars grow to thousands and millions in the night sky. Sometimes they would watch the moon rising, or listen to the wind howling and wonder if it was trying to tell them a little story. But no; they would yawn and yawn, till they fell asleep without even a dream. Can you imagine – the whole world without any stories or dreams! It was terrible. Mothers and grandmothers tried hard to find a story or two for their little ones, but there were none.

One day Zenzele told his wife that she should go out into the forest and plains nearby and that maybe there she would meet

animals who knew some stories. With her heart full of hope, Mazanendaba set off on her search.

The first animal she met was the Hare, who was a trickster even back then. He smiled his toothy smile and said: 'I know lots of stories. For instance, I could tell you a story about … eeh … eeh. Oh! I'm in such a hurry! Next time I see you I'll tell you.' Liar! Hare did not know any stories.

Then she met a big mother Baboon, who stood clumsily in front of Mazanendaba and said: 'Ha! What are you saying? Are you telling me that human children are more problematic than our children? You give them a house to stay in, clothes to wear and food to eat, and on top of that they still want stories? *Hayi!* I'm lucky I'm not a human mother!'

Next, Mazanendaba met a Mamba Snake. Mamba was very shy: 'I don't even know what a story is,' she whispered in a hoarse voice, and disappeared into the green grass.

The Owl was very cross with Mazanendaba: 'You know I sleep in the day time – where do you think I get stories from? Please woman, leave me alone. *Woo, Woo!*' And he went back to sleep.

Mazanendaba was beginning to lose hope when she met a large grey Elephant, who smiled and said: 'I do not know any stories myself, but I suggest that you go and ask the Eagle. Eagles are the ones who fly up highest, they are the ones who dare to look at the sun, maybe they know some stories.'

Thanking the Elephant, the woman went back home and rested for the day. The next morning, she was sitting in front of her house when she saw a Fish Eagle, who had just caught a fish. She ran down to the beach shouting: 'Hey Eagle, please do not fly away. I need to talk to you!' The Eagle was so startled that he dropped his fish. With angry eyes he stared at Mazanendaba and said: 'You have made me drop my lunch, Woman!'

'I know, I know – please forgive me. But I badly need your help,' said Mazanendaba.

'What could I possibly help you with?' demanded Eagle.

'You see, I need stories for my children. I have looked everywhere and Elephant said you are the only one who can help me. Please – even one story from your family would help, oh Wise Eagle.' she said.

As soon as he heard 'Wise Eagle', he smiled a big smile and said: 'How very kind of you to call me "Wise Eagle". Well, my friend Dolphin tells me there are no stories here in this world. They are all kept in an underwater Kingdom below the Ocean. That is where the Spirit King and Queen live with the Spirit People. Dolphin can take you there anytime you want.'

Mazanendaba was so excited she wanted to throw herself into the rough sea right there and then. But Eagle said: 'Wait! Don't do that, you don't even know which Dolphin I'm talking about.'

Wise Eagle flew away. Much later he came back and landed in front of the woman, saying: 'Look over there and tell me who you see.'

'Oh – *sawubona* Dolphin!' greeted the woman excitedly. To her left she saw a friendly-looking dolphin who was eyeing her with great interest. Mazanendaba was very impressed by that kind and friendly face, which looked like the face of someone who had been to all kinds of secret and magical places.

Dolphin smiled and told her to climb on his back so that they could go to the underwater Kingdom while it was still daylight. The woman did as he said. She held on tightly to the large fin and under a big wave they went: '*Tyumbu! Bloop bloop bloooop!*' All the way down to the bottom of the Ocean. They arrived at a place of amazing beauty. It was filled with brilliant light, even though there was no sun and no moon. Mazanendaba looked at the eyes of the Spirit People and saw that the light was coming from them. They all had eyes like stars. And their faces and bodies were very beautiful, with colours like green, purple, orange, yellow, blue and many others. They welcomed her to their home, and as they spoke, it was as if wonderful music suddenly filled the whole place. Mazanendaba closed her eyes and listened to the beautiful sound of their musical voices. Dolphin had to laugh when he saw how impressed she was.

Then Mazanendaba was taken to meet the Spirit King and Queen. She sat respectfully in front of them and asked them for stories.

'We can give you all the stories your heart desires. But what will you bring for us from your home in return?' asked the Spirit King.

Mazanendaba could not think of anything … nothing that seemed good enough for a Spirit King and Queen. Then the Spirit Queen smiled and said: 'It would please us most if you could bring us a picture of your home, yourself, your husband and children.

We cannot come up to visit you where you live, but we would like to know where these stories are going to.'

Mazanendaba did not waste any more time. She climbed on the Dolphin's back and up they went through the water and back to the beach. Zenzele, her husband, was waiting there with the children, not knowing when Mazanendaba would return. She said goodbye to the Dolphin and arranged to meet him again after three days, at sunrise. Then she sat with her family and told them everything she had seen and heard in the underwater Kingdom. Most importantly, she told them about the picture the Spirit Queen had asked for. Zenzele knew exactly what to do. The next morning he took a big flat piece of wood and started to carve the picture of their house. Then he carved the face of his wife, and this he enjoyed a lot. He added in his own face and then those of the children – the naughty boy with the smiling eyes, the little girl with the lovely smile, the tall boy with the long legs … all of them! When he thought he had finished, guess who came to help? Eagle! He also wanted to be in the picture. So Zenzele carved him in as well, just above the house.

On the third morning at sunrise, Zenzele took the picture carving, put it on his wife's back and tied it tightly with a leather strap. Then Mazanendaba went down to the beach where the Dolphin was already waiting. She climbed onto his back and under a big wave they went: 'Tyumbu! Bloop bloop bloooop!' all the way down to the bottom of the Ocean.

The Spirit People were overjoyed with the picture carving. They all crowded around for a closer look, lighting up the carving with their star-like eyes and making musical praises with their melodious voices. The King and Queen were very pleased indeed! They handed Mazanendaba a necklace made of tiny shells as a thank you present to her husband for all his hard work. Then they gave her a big, pink, shiny and magical-looking shell. They told her that it contained countless stories. Hundreds and thousands of stories were kept inside that shell, so many that each time she listened to the shell she would hear a new story – every single time. Mazanendaba thanked them from the bottom of her heart. She said goodbye and, holding the magical story shell lovingly to her chest, she let Dolphin take her back to the beach, where her family was waiting anxiously for her return.

But they were not the only people waiting for her. All the people of their village, as well as from other villages near and far, had come to welcome her back and hear some of the stories she had brought with her. Mamba Snake was there too and so were Hare, Owl, mother Baboon with her children, Elephant and Wise Eagle. It was late afternoon and the colours of the sunset glowed brilliantly in the western sky. The large crowd sat down on the beach and waited for Mazanendaba to tell them a story.

She picked up the magical story shell, put it to her ear and listened for a few seconds. Then she began: '*Kwesukesukela* …' which means, 'it happened a long time ago …'

'*Cosi!*' everyone replied, meaning, 'we are ready to listen'. And so the first story in the world was told. When Mazanendaba had finished, the listeners all begged: 'Another one please!' And so she told them story after story. Every sunset from then on it was story time, and those stories went from village to village, from country to country, to all the continents of the world. Until my grandmother heard some of those stories, and now I am sharing them with you.

Cosi, cosi, iyaphela

HERE I REST MY STORY

HOW TORTOISE WON RESPECT

Illustrations by Junior Valentim

IT IS SAID THAT a long, long time ago, when the world was still young and life was very different to the way it is today, animals were not such good hunters. In those days, Lion was King of the animals, and every single animal respected him. He was mighty and strong and did not have to talk very loudly, for his word was law and that was that.

But the animals had a problem. They did not have a place of their own where they could grow food. So they had to go to the gardens of human beings to steal whatever vegetables they wanted. This was often very dangerous, because if they were caught, they ended up in a human's stew pot! In fact, this happened far too often, until one day King Lion could stand it no longer. So he called a big meeting of all his subjects. He told them it was time they moved to another place where there were no humans, where they could plant their own food and live a more respectable life.

'*Elethu! Elethu!* We all agree!' was the response from every animal. Cheetah was sent to go and steal some tools from the humans, which he did with pleasure. Well known trickster, Nogwaja the Hare, was only too happy to go and steal some seeds for his King. All the animals then set off to find a new place where they could live and grow their food in peace. The fast ones like Cheetah and Jackal led the way. In the middle were the King and other big animals like Buffalo, Elephant, Rhino and Giraffe. At the back were the slow moving ones like

Chameleon and Tortoise. The sun was hot and the journey was long. But at last Cheetah shouted at the top of his voice: 'O King, we have found a place. It looks very fertile and there is a lake where we can drink water!'

'But are there any human beings in sight?' was the question from Lion.

'No, not one,' replied Cheetah.

So at last the animals had found a home. They worked very hard in the following days, ploughing the land and planting their seeds. Soon enough the rains came. In time the large garden yielded delicious carrots, pumpkins, cabbages, sweet potatoes and lots more. The animals had a great time eating their food, drinking at the lake, and enjoying glorious sunsets, without any humans to chase or kill them.

Then one day, Zebra woke up early with his best friend Ostrich. They were extremely hungry, so they set off for the garden. But when they got there, they found that all the food was gone; not a sweet potato, not a leaf of cabbage, not a blade of grass was left! Even the lake was almost empty. Someone or something had come in the middle of the night and stolen everything.

Suddenly a shadow seemed to fall across the rising sun, and the sky went dark. When Zebra and Ostrich looked up, they saw a huge mountain of an animal. It was like ten elephants put together. Its skin was moist, greyish brown and smelly. Its eyes were huge and green and slimy. Its nostrils were like two big caves with hot air coming out of them. Its mouth was the biggest cave of all, full of sharp grey teeth. Poor terrified Zebra tried to be brave, and so he asked this monster who he was and what he wanted.

'I AM GONGQONGQO!' bellowed the monster, 'THE ONE WHO SWALLOWS BUFFALOES ALIVE, HORNS AND ALL. WHO ARE YOU, LITTLE ZEBRA, TO ASK ME SUCH STUPID QUESTIONS?'

Zebra and Ostrich were filled with fear and rushed off to tell everyone what they had seen and heard. The other animals were just as frightened, but Lion, their King, said he would deal with Gongqongqo. He told them not to be afraid. Lion's muscles were shining, his tail was up in the air and his golden mane looked magnificent as the morning sun danced on it. But when he arrived in the garden and saw how very large this monster was, he knew he did not stand a chance of winning a fight. He decided to roar as loudly as he could to scare the monster off.

'Who do you think you are, coming into my kingdom and stealing the food my subjects have worked so hard for? Get away from here and never come back!' roared the King of the animals.

Gongqongqo opened his monstrous mouth and answered: 'I AM GONGQONGQO! HE WHO SWALLOWS BUFFALOES ALIVE, HORNS AND ALL. AS FOR YOU, LITTLE CAT, I WILL HAVE YOU FOR A SNACK!'

King Lion's tail disappeared between his legs, and he ran as fast as he could back to his subjects to tell them it was time to move on to a new place, for this monster was far worse than even human beings. 'Elethu! We all agree!' was the response, Buffalo's voice shouting loudest of all. But Tortoise had other ideas. She declared that she was going to deal with the monster in her own way. The other animals laughed at her. They said she was crazy to think that someone as small as her could face up to such a creature. But Lion told everyone to keep quiet. He listened carefully to what Tortoise had to say. Then he took one of the sharp little axes that Cheetah had stolen from the humans, and gave it to Tortoise to hide under her shell. He wished her good luck.

Tortoise set off at her slow pace to face Gongqongqo. She looked tiny as she stood in front of the huge monster. But bravely she shouted at the top of her voice: 'Heyi wena, who do you think you are? Do you think we are scared of you? No, we are not. Also, I must tell you that you are very ugly, and furthermore, you smell. So get away from here. Hamba – get away!'

The monster could not believe what he was hearing. 'I AM GONGQONGQO I TELL YOU, AND I AM NOT GOING TO GO AWAY. INSTEAD, I WILL TAKE YOU, TINY TORTOISE, TOSS YOU UNDER MY TONGUE, AND FORGET ALL ABOUT YOU!' And sure enough, his long, slimy, yellow tongue came out and – 'Illwabi' – Tortoise disappeared inside that awful mouth!

Then, quick as a flash, Tortoise took out the sharp axe from under her shell and started to chop at the monster's tongue. Chop, chop, chop. The monster thought he was getting a headache and groaned loudly. What on earth was going on? What was that silly little tortoise up to, he wondered, shaking his head violently. But Tortoise did not stop. She continued to chop away at the tongue until it fell off, and then she chopped her way across the neck. Gongqongqo made loud, thundering noises, scaring the whole countryside and forest for miles around. Finally, it happened; Gongqongqo fell down dead!

The smiling Tortoise climbed out of the gate she had opened on the side of the monster's neck and, holding the little axe high, she called out: 'It is I, it is I, little Tortoise. I killed Gongqongqo!'

All the other animals came out of their hiding places and cheered for the brave Tortoise, calling her the cleverest of them all.

King Lion declared her the bravest and most respected citizen in his Kingdom … well, after him, of course!

Cosi, cosi, iyaphela

HERE I REST MY STORY

KASANKO'S DREAM

Illustrations by Lalelani Mbhele

ONCE THERE LIVED A MAN called Kasanko, who was a very well-liked and respected ironmonger. He made all sorts of wonderful things out of iron – tools and special metal boxes, unusual bracelets, necklaces and rings. Most of all, he enjoyed making things that others could not make. Kasanko took great pride in his work and everything he made was so special to him that he sometimes found it hard to part with his things. His work was always in demand and he was often asked to make special items for the King.

Whenever King Dabulamanzi called him to the Great Palace, Kasanko was never sure what to expect. The King often got bored and sometimes, just to amuse himself, he would ask people to do the most impossible things for him. When they failed, he chased them out of his Kingdom. So far, Kasanko had escaped this fate. He was one man the King really respected, so people said.

One day the King's messenger arrived to summon Kasanko to the palace, instructing him to be there first thing the following morning. Kasanko wondered what awaited him.

He rose early the next day, and went to the Great Palace, where King Dabulamanzi was waiting for him. He told Kasanko that he wanted him to do something very special for him. The King then led him outside, to a large pile of broken iron chairs, spears, knives and all kinds of old tools that were no longer used. He told Kasanko that he wanted him to take these things away and out of them, make a person. Yes, a person – with a mind to think, a voice to speak and lungs to breathe. In every way just like a human, except that he would have an iron body which would never grow old.

Kasanko stood shocked and dismayed by the King's request. 'I must tell you right now that I can't perform this task for you. It is impossible, O King, to make a living person out of iron. So you might as well kill me right now!'

But the King just laughed at his words and said: 'Oh you are so modest Kasanko! Of course you can do this thing. I know your special talent. You can do anything

t your mind to. I am counting on you – so please, don't disappoint me.'

sanko tried to protest further. But the King would not listen to anything he said.

ad, he ordered his servants to carry the big pile of scrap metal off to Kasanko's

hou..e. The whole village stared in open-mouthed amazement as the royal party arrived bearing the mountain of old iron junk. Kasanko's wife took one look at her husband's distraught face and knew that something very bad was happening.

'If I was a child, I would throw myself on the ground and cry!' Kasanko told her. 'The King has gone too far this time. He has ordered me to make a living being out of scrap metal – one who can think, speak and breathe like a human. Am I God, I ask myself?'

'Please Baba, calm down, calm down,' begged his wife. 'How does the King expect you to do this impossible thing?'

'You see all that scrap iron outside? Well that is for the body. How he expects me to do the rest he did not say. But if I fail, I am a dead man.'

Kasanko was furious with the arrogant King. He kept his anger to himself, however, while he tried to work out what to do next. Days went by, but his usually clever imagination did not come to his rescue. His wife was desperately worried about him.

One day, Kasanko went walking alone in the hills. He sat down on a hilltop to rest, grateful for the cool breeze on his hot face as he tried to think of some way out of his dilemma. All at once, he saw someone coming up the path towards him. It was a man called Senzo, who the people of the village called 'crazy Senzo'. This was because he talked to himself, laughed out loud at nothing, and sometimes did strange things. But since he never harmed anyone, everyone left him alone. Sometimes, people said, he could help you laugh on a sad day.

Kasanko had always liked Senzo. He called the man over to come and sit beside him. Soon, he found himself pouring out all his troubles. Senzo listened quietly to his story, and sat frowning in thought for a long while. Then he said: 'If I were you, Kasanko, this is what I would say to the King. I would tell him that in order to complete your task and make a living iron man, there are certain things you need. To make the joints move and the tongue speak – 50 bags of human hair. To make the heart beat and the mind think – 100 litres of human tears.'

Kasanko couldn't contain his joy. What a brilliant solution! Match one crazy idea with another! He shook Senzo's hand, hugged him, kissed him and thanked him over and over again. 'Oh you in your madness are the smartest of us all. You have just saved my life! Thank you, Senzo, my friend. Thank you.'

Kasanko rushed off home, quickly changed his clothes and got ready to go to the Great Palace to see the King. For the first time in days there was a smile on his face, and he even had an appetite for the food his wife had prepared for him.

At the Palace, the King welcomed him and sat down to hear what progress had been made on the creation of his living man. Kasanko cleared his throat and said: 'My respected King, I have been working day and night to make you your living iron person. I am nearly there, but to finish the job, I need two things from you.'

'Whatever they are, tell me and I will make sure you get them immediately!' cried King Dabulamanzi, beside himself with excitement.

'What I require is not simple,' cautioned Kasanko. 'But without these things, I cannot bring this iron man to life. To make the joints move and the tongue speak, I need 50 bags of human hair.'

'Easy, easy,' cried the King. 'What else do you need, Kasanko, speak freely.'

'To make the heart beat and the mind think, I need 100 litres of human tears.'

The King's smile faded. He called his servants and told them what Kasanko needed. He ordered them to shave the heads of as many people as was necessary to fill 50 bags with hair. The servants were puzzled, but they went to obey the King's orders.

'You can go home now, Kasanko. The bags of hair will be delivered to your house in the next few days and the 100 litres of tears will soon follow.'

And so the King made his promise. But Kasanko could see that Dabulamanzi was not as excited as before. Kasanko said goodbye and left.

A few days later, the 50 bags of hair arrived on Kasanko's doorstep. The King's soldiers had gone from village to village shaving everybody – men, women and children – on the King's orders. Then the news spread all over the kingdom that the King needed 100 litres of tears to help make a living iron man. Big clay pots were brought for people to cry into. As commanded, everyone walked around looking very sad. Some people managed to cry as instructed, but others just could not cry on command.

So the King ordered his soldiers to beat the people up and make them cry. Yes, thousands of people were reduced to tears by the painful beatings. This soon had them fighting back. Even the soldiers hated the stupidity of what they were being ordered to do. In the end, it did not help very much anyway, because it was almost impossible to collect the tears. People wiped their tears away from habit. Or the hot African sun dried the tears on their cheeks as fast as they flowed.

King Dabulamanzi was furious. He just didn't know what more he could do to squeeze the necessary tears out of his subjects. How could he tell Kasanko that he had failed to keep his part of the bargain? He was greatly tormented by the thought that he would not receive his living iron man, the miracle he had so desperately desired.

Then it dawned on the King what was really going on. He realised that Kasanko was asking the impossible from him, just as he had asked the impossible from Kasanko. The ironmonger had matched one crazy idea with another. There was nothing the King could do except swallow his pride and tell Kasanko to forget the whole thing.

All that night the King lay sleepless, thinking many troubled thoughts. The next day, he went straight to Kasanko's house and humbly apologised to him.

16

'You have made me realise, Kasanko, what a cruel and thoughtless King I have been to my subjects. I have given impossible commands and harshly punished those who failed to carry them out. How can I begin to ask for forgiveness from you and the many others that I have hurt? To make it up to you, you may ask me for anything that your heart desires. Anything.'

'It has always been my dream that this village of ours would become a centre of excellence, known far and wide for the quality of its crafts,' Kasanko told him. 'What my heart desires most of all is to start a school, where I can pass on my skills to others and teach them to put the best of themselves into the beautiful things they make.'

'I will see to it that you get everything you need,' promised the King.

And he was as good as his word. In time, Kasanko's village became famous throughout the land for the excellent crafts it produced. From far and wide people sent their children to Kasanko's school to learn the skills of weaving, carving, pottery and ironmongery. Kasanko was very proud of his school and the achievements of its talented pupils. And remember 'crazy' Senzo? Well, he became one of Kasanko's closest friends. He was known from then on as Senzo the Wise, and treated with a lot more respect by everyone.

As for King Dabulamanzi, he learnt to respect his people. He stopped dishing out impossible commands that no one could carry out and became one of the most popular Kings of all time.

Cosi, cosi, iyaphela

HERE I REST MY STORY

JABULANI
AND THE LION

Illustrations by Lalelani Mbhele

A LONG TIME AGO, there was a young boy called Jabulani, who lived with his mother and father. His family had many cattle and Jabulani was a good herdboy. He loved eating *amasi,* which is curdled milk. It was his favourite meal on a hot summer's day. But his best time of year was winter, just after all the fields had been harvested. The cattle were then allowed to go into the fields to eat mealie stalks. They did not move very fast since there was so much to eat in one place. So the boys were free to play for as long as they wanted to. For some of them, the days felt long and empty. But not for Jabulani. He did many things with his time. He loved making clay oxen and playing quietly on the riverbank, enjoying the winter sun. He also loved hunting for field mice, singing in time with the rhythmic thudding of his hunting stick in the tall dry grass.

Jabulani was walking along and singing like this one morning, when he suddenly stopped dead in his tracks. He thought he had heard something. He listened hard. It was someone calling urgently for help. From the sound of that deep voice Jabulani imagined that it must belong to a big man. He ran to see. And there was indeed someone very big and in distress – a Lion caught in a hunter's trap. His eyes were full of pleading and he looked like only a shadow of the great King of the Jungle that we all hear about. Jabulani felt sorry for the Lion, but he was also scared of what would happen to him once the Lion was free.

'*Ngisize bo Mfana,* please help me, boy!' implored the Lion.

'I want to help you – but won't you kill me once you are free from that trap?' asked Jabulani.

'Of course not! What do you take me for? How could I kill someone who saves my life? Please – I'm dying!'

'Lion, you must really promise me that you will not hurt me,' insisted Jabulani.

'All right, all right, I promise. If you free me I will be your friend and I will teach you to hunt like a Lion. We will go everywhere together.'

Oh, Jabulani liked that promise! He thought to himself: 'That would be so great! Other boys have cats or dogs for pets, but I will have a Lion for my friend. Everyone will envy me – I can just see it!'

So the boy freed the Lion from the trap. The Lion was very tired and thirsty. He asked Jabulani what his name was and then he thanked him and said: 'We should find a river so I can have a drink. Please, my friend.'

So the two new friends went down to the river together. The Lion had a long, long drink, as if he wanted to drink the whole river! Jabulani smiled as he watched him. Then the Lion opened one eye and looked at the boy: 'Nice leg …' He looked up some more: 'Nice arm … nice boy altogether!' Suddenly the Lion grabbed Jabulani's hand and said: 'Jabulani, I am not thirsty anymore, but I am very hungry!'

'Then we must go hunting,' said Jabulani.

'Why should I go hunting when there is food right here in front of me? I will eat *you*, my friend,' replied the Lion threateningly.

Jabulani knew he had made a big mistake in trusting the Lion. He was gripped with fear and pleaded with the Lion: 'But … but you promised that you would not …'

'*Heyi wena*, I cannot eat promises. I am hungry now and food is standing right in front of me,' said the Lion, baring his teeth.

'Oh please, Lion, wait a little. Let's go and ask the other animals if it is right to eat someone who has saved your life.'

'All right, suit yourself. But you know they will side with me.'

So the two went off to find an animal they could ask. The first one was an old Cow, standing chewing grass and ruminating. They greeted her and told her the story. Her response was: '*Mooo*, I do not like humans. All my life I have worked hard pulling the plough, tilling their land, producing milk for them, and now that I am old and weak, they are preparing to kill and eat me. Please, King of the Jungle, eat the boy!'

'No! No! We cannot listen to one unhappy old Cow. Let's ask someone else,' begged Jabulani.

The Donkey they asked was not on Jabulani's side either. After relating all his unhappiness with humans, he too said: 'Please, King of the Jungle, eat the boy!'

The other animals they consulted, and even birds like the Ostriches, all said the same thing: 'Please, King of the Jungle, eat the boy!'

Now Jabulani was sweating and close to tears. The Lion, by contrast, was smiling broadly.

'What did I tell you? You have to admit they are all right. After all, who put the trap that caught me there in the first place …?'

It was beginning to look as if Jabulani was never going to see his parents again, or watch another daybreak. At that point, they met a Jackal. He was walking along slowly, mischief in his eyes as he watched the two companions. He chuckled in disbelief and asked: 'What is this I see? King Lion and a young boy, walking around together and looking like they are actually friends? How did that happen? Please tell me!'

'Yes, we are supposed to be friends, but now Lion here wants to eat me. Please Jackal, help me,' pleaded the boy.

'But how can I help you? Oh do tell me more!' the Jackal said.

'You see, this Lion was caught in a hunter's trap. He was in great pain and would have died if I had not come along and saved him. He promised to be my friend and said that he would teach me to hunt like a Lion, but now he wants to eat me …' cried Jabulani.

'Wait a minute here! My King, the powerful and feared Bhubesi, caught in a stupid hunter's trap? No, try another story – I hate lies!' The Jackal looked very disbelieving.

'The boy is telling the truth. He did save my life. But now I'm starving and need to eat, so don't waste any more of my time.' The Lion was clearly very irritated by all this talk.

'Well, I must be very slow, because I find this story totally unbelievable,' said the Jackal. 'Why don't you take me to the place and show me exactly what happened? Then I will have no choice but to accept that you must eat the boy!' Jackal acted quite confused by it all.

So they all walked to the place where the trap was, and at Jackal's suggestion, they acted out the scene just as it had happened. Quite unsuspectingly, the Lion climbed right back into the trap. Then Jackal asked the boy to secure it just the way it was before, so

he could *really* see how it had happened.

'Are you satisfied now?' growled the Lion irritably. 'Come on, tell the boy to free me again. I'm tired of your games.'

'Yes, I'm satisfied,' cunning Jackal said. 'Well, I must say that looks very good indeed. Jabulani, your mother must be missing you. Run along home boy – *run!*'

Jabulani could not believe his luck. Stammering his thanks to the Jackal, he ran home as fast as his feet could carry him.

Then Jackal turned to look at the Lion, who was so furious that sparks of fire flew from his eyes.

'How dare you let my meat go!' Lion roared.

'Well, well now. It looks like you will just have to eat your promises. Goodbye King Bhubesi, you most powerful beast of all.'

And with a mischievous chuckle, Jackal walked away.

Cosi, cosi, iyaphela

HERE I REST MY STORY

KHETHIWE,
QUEEN OF IMBIRA

Illustrations by Jeannie Kinsler

NO GIRL IN THIS LAND shall play imbira.

'No, no, no! I said *no* girl in this land shall play imbira!'

'Yes, you heard me right. No girl must play imbira.'

These are the words that Khethiwe listened to all through the years that she was growing up. They made her very sad. More than anything, she longed to be allowed to play the imbira. An imbira is a very special instrument, one that plays sacred music to call good spirits back to the home. It is also called a kalimba, a sanza, or a thumb piano. In Khethiwe's land, only men and boys were allowed to play such a sacred instrument. This was the law of the land and all the other girls seemed to accept it. All except Khethiwe. Her dream was to one day own this beautiful instrument for herself. Because it was forbidden for girls to play it, she knew that no one would help her to learn how to play the imbira. She would have to teach herself.

Khethiwe lived with her mother and father in a homestead near the river. She was a quiet and thoughtful child, who loved helping with all the chores at home. All day she worked happily around the house and when she was finished, she would head for the big pool in the river, where she loved to go swimming. She always chose to go down there in the late afternoon, just before sunset. For at that hour, there is a magical golden light that washes over the land, making everyone and everything look beautiful. This is the time that the people of Africa call *'libantu bahle* – the time of beautiful people'.

This was Khethiwe's favourite time to swim in the river. Sometimes, some of the other girls would come and join her, but mostly she went there alone. One day, while she was playing quietly by herself at the river, enjoying the peace and beauty of *'libantu bahle'*, an amazing thing happened. Looking into the pool, she noticed movement under the water. Big ripples spread out, coming closer and closer towards her. Then, out of the river, a mysterious hand emerged, shining and golden. Khethiwe was very afraid. She had never seen such a thing in her life before. Then she saw that the hand was holding something out to her. It was an imbira! A beautiful imbira, dripping wet but otherwise in good shape. Hardly able to believe her eyes, Khethiwe accepted it, stammering her thanks to the hand and its unseen owner.

Quickly she dried herself, got dressed as fast as she could and ran all the way home with her secret gift hidden carefully in her shawl. The next day she did her chores as usual, helping her parents at home until the day was spent. And then, just as she always did, she went down to the river at her favourite time – the time of the beautiful people. But Khethiwe was no longer interested in swimming. She was looking for a safe hiding place where she could sit undisturbed and learn to play her instrument.

She found a cave that looked out onto the running water of the river, with a big, flat rock overhanging it. It was as if she had found her own personal veranda. Khethiwe made herself comfortable, took up her imbira, and hesitantly plucked the strings:

'Qim, qim, qim!' she tried awkwardly to play. It was not easy at all! Try as she might, she could not produce the music she heard in her head. But she kept on with her secret practising, returning to the cave every sundown, plucking those strings until her fingers were sore. *Hayi*, it was frustrating!

'Maybe it is true that men are cleverer than we girls are …' she said to herself. But no – that she would never believe! The thought made her even more determined to succeed. She practised and practised, spending hours by herself in the secret cave. And then it happened; one day, she decided to stop trying so hard and let the imbira guide her. She started to relax with her playing. And slowly, she felt it coming …

'*Hayaya qim – qim, hayaya qim – qim!* Oh Yes!'

Khethiwe was beside herself with joy. She couldn't stop grinning as she felt the lovely rhythms wash over her and the sound of the sacred music filled her ears. This was very good! At long last she could play the beautiful music of her ancestors.

From that day onwards, Khethiwe listened for inspiring sounds wherever she went, sounds she could use for her music. The bird songs she heard provided new melodies for her instrument. The gurgling waters of the river gave her new rhythms. She could feel the music of her ancestors pulsing in her blood, beating in her bones, in her marrow! It made her so happy when she played her imbira. But she still had to keep it a secret from everyone, which was very hard.

Every year in late July, at the end of harvest celebration, all the people in the land gathered at the King's kraal to celebrate. The boys and men who could play the imbira got together in a large circle and played beautiful melodies. Those in the crowd who felt like dancing dressed up in their traditional clothes and went into the middle of the circle to dance.

Khethiwe wrapped a cloth around her imbira and hid it carefully where nobody would find it. She put on her most special clothes and beads, stepped out of her home looking extremely lovely, and went to join the dancers at the celebration. And hey, could she dance! Her limbs seemed to flow like water to the beautiful imbira sounds. She moved her body so gracefully that people couldn't take their eyes off her. Some called out: '*Heyi, heyi, heyi! Uyadela umfazi owazala leya ntombi, hala-la!* Lucky is the mother who gave birth to that child!'

But others were jealous, and they said harshly: '*Mpff!* That one thinks she is a queen!'

The King was at the celebration that day, sitting there in his special place, watching everyone enjoying themselves. He was having a very good time, glad to see his people so happy. He overheard the different comments about Khethiwe and thought to himself that she was the best imbira dancer of all.

It wasn't long after this event when the nice old King fell seriously ill. Everyone in the kingdom was very upset, because he was a kind and popular ruler. Many different kinds of healing potions were brought to the royal hut, and the King drank them all, but he did not get better. Ancestral ceremonies were performed, but nothing helped. He only got worse.

The elders began to accept that their King did not have very long to live. They went to the King's kraal to be with him on the last part of his journey, for they all agreed that his final day had come, though when exactly he would

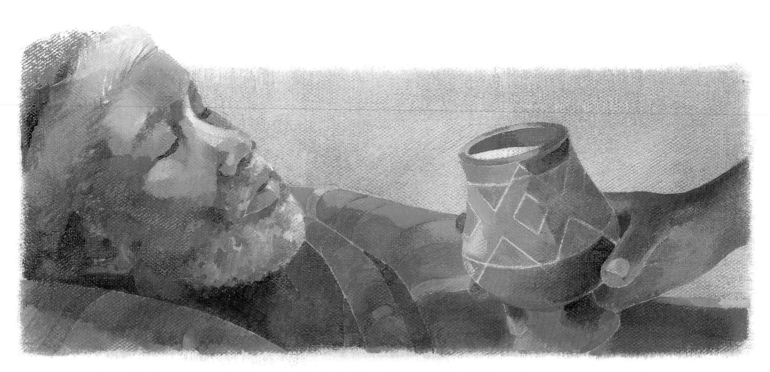

draw his last breath they couldn't decide. Some said: 'He's only got one more hour to live,' while others said: 'No, no, he's only got one more second.'

On that same day, at the special time when the people say '*libantu bahle*', Khethiwe was in her cave by the river. Sadly she sat playing her sacred imbira, wishing with all her heart that some miracle would happen to save the dying King's life. Suddenly, she had a strong feeling that she should go and see him. She hurried from the cave, taking her imbira with her. This time, she did not bother to hide the instrument, but continued playing it as she walked along. All who saw her were shocked.

'*Mameshane, Mameshane!*' they exclaimed. 'What is this? A girl playing an imbira? We shall be cursed!'

But Khethiwe did not even hear them. As if some strong force was pushing her from behind, she walked faster and faster towards the King's kraal. The elders who were gathered there heard the sound of the imbira coming towards them out of the distance. Then they saw Khethiwe at the door. At the sight of the King lying on his deathbed, she fell onto her knees in respect. Still on her knees, she crawled over to where he was lying and, taking up her instrument, she played it next to the King's ear … softly at first, then louder and more loudly still. Then she started to sing: '*Siyayi biza imimoya, yaba ngasekho*. We are calling on the spirits of those long gone.'

As Khethiwe continued to sing and play her beautiful melodies, the elders heard the sound of other imbiras and other voices joining in with hers. It was as if an invisible crowd of imbira players filled the room. The only one they could see was Khethiwe.

The sick King opened his eyes. He sat up in his bed and looked around the room. He lifted his finger and pointed towards the walls, calling out the names of the invisible people. Yes, he could see the faces of Kings and Queens long dead. He saw his grandparents and great grandparents looking back at him. They were all saying the same thing: 'Keep on living, *qhubeka uphile!* Keep on living, *qhubeka uphile!*'

Then the King's eyes fell on Khethiwe and he smiled.

'Khethiwe,' he said, 'you are the Chosen One, just like your name. Your beautiful imbira playing has summoned the ancestors. Thank you for saving my life! From this day on, I command that not just every boy but every girl in this land shall be free to play the music of our ancestors. Play your imbira, Khethiwe. Don't stop. Keep on playing, *qhubeka udlale!* Keep on playing, *qhubeka udlale!*'

Khethiwe was overjoyed to hear the King's words. And did she play! The elders didn't try to stop her. They were just so relieved and happy to see their King restored to health and in such good spirits. So, as you can guess, at the next end of harvest celebration, when all the imbira players gathered together to play for the crowd, Khethiwe was right there with them. It made her very happy to be able to take her rightful place among them. And other little girls were there too, following her example and trying hard to play. From then on, there was no holding them back. The King of the land himself had given the command: 'Keep on playing, *qhubeka udlale!*'

Everyone agreed that it was the best end of harvest celebration in living memory.

Cosi, cosi, iyaphela

HERE I REST MY STORY

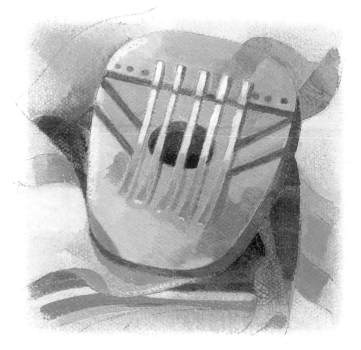

LION THATCHES HIS ROOF

Illustrations by Kim Longhurst

ONCE, A LONG TIME AGO, Lion was chosen as King of the Beasts. He was a proud and powerful King, feared and respected by all his subjects. One day Lion decided he was much too important to be sleeping in the open veld under the stars. After all, he was King of the Beasts – why should he sleep outside like any ordinary animal?

Early one morning Lion went out and collected building materials, then set about building his house. When the walls were done, he collected thatch grass and started on the roof.

Soon, there was only one small section left to finish. Lion decided on a special way to celebrate. He caught and killed a fat Kudu and cooked it in two pots – slowly, slowly, until it was very soft and succulent. Then he put out the fire and climbed onto the roof to finish the thatching. The King of the Beasts was in good spirits as he worked. He could not wait to sit inside his new house and celebrate with a pot of really delicious meat all to himself. He felt like the most important King who ever lived.

Not very far from where Lion's new house was, Nogwaja the Hare was walking to the river when he suddenly smelt something really delicious cooking. He stopped, sniffed this way and that way. Ha! His nose told him where to go. Soon, he was standing in front of King Lion's house and up there on the roof was Lion, humming a happy tune as he worked.

'*Nkosi enkulu, ngiyakhuleka!* Great King, I greet you,' said Nogwaja.

'What do you want here?' demanded Lion.

'I don't mean to be rude, my King, but I feel it is very sad that you have to work so hard when you are King of the Beasts. It is terrible that we did not come to assist you from the start. Please, let me help you finish the remaining work. It would be a great honour for me,' said the Hare, thinking about how he could trick the King and get to eat some of the meat in the pots.

'Well, come on then,' agreed Lion. 'Come inside the hut and help me with the thatching. Climb on that chair and take hold of the needle when I push it through from above, then push it back up through the grass and return it to me.'

'And hurry!' Lion ordered, thinking to himself: 'This way I can do the job in half the time and then eat Hare as part of my supper.'

The two animals worked in silence for a while until Nogwaja realised that the King's tail was dangling down inside the hut. His sharp mind told him: 'Hey, I can tie the King's tail to the roof very tightly and jump down to eat his meat.'

And this is exactly what Nogwaja did. Each time the needle came back in again, he first wound it around Lion's tail, so that the tail was stitched into the section of grass, before he sent the needle back up again. Soon Lion asked: 'Nogwaja, why is my tail itching? What are you up to?'

'Oh, please let me scratch it for you,' said the Hare. He scratched the tail and tied it up even more tightly now that he had permission to touch it. When he was sure that it was very securely tied and Lion could not get down, Nogwaja jumped down and went straight for the meat pots. '*Heyi wena* – you, Big Ears – what do you think you are doing?' thundered the King.

'Please, you don't have to be so angry. I just want to know what fat juicy meat this is,' replied Nogwaja, taking the lid off the bigger pot.

'That meat belongs to me, your King, so leave it alone!'

'And what about this one here in the other pot?'

'That, too, belongs to me, so don't even think that it could be for little creatures like you,' said Lion, becoming really furious.

'Well, I don't care in the least whose meat it is, because I plan to eat all I want!' said the naughty Hare – and started helping himself to the meat. He even praised the King for being such a good cook!

'What do you think you are doing, Nogwaja! I will kill you right now!' roared Lion, and tried to jump down, but he could not. His tail was very tightly tied to the roof thatch.

It made him even angrier when he thought how hard he had worked to make this such a special day. He roared till his voice was hoarse. But he could do nothing except watch as Nogwaja feasted on his well-cooked meat. Nogwaja polished off all that he could eat. Then he walked away, cheekily waving goodbye to Lion and thanking him for his kindness.

Lion was forced to stay sitting on the roof of his new house in the hot sun until much later, when some of the other animals came and saved him from up there. But they ran for their lives as soon as they had freed him … just in case! He thanked them politely, however, and went to eat the leftovers of his feast.

Lion vowed that one day very soon, he would catch Nogwaja and teach him a lesson he would never forget. Every night that he spent in his house, Lion dreamed of catching Nogwaja and eating him up.

As for Nogwaja, that night, after he ate Lion's potful of meat, he had a stomach ache so severe it was as if mad Zebras were kicking inside his belly. The Hare moaned, groaned and cried. And from that day on he decided that he would become a vegetarian, and never touch meat again. He also had the punishment of knowing that Lion would be after him day and night, for the rest of his short little life.

Cosi, cosi, iyaphela

HERE I REST MY STORY

33

LEOPARD'S GIFT

Illustrations by Kalle Becker

THERE WAS A TIME when people lived to be very old without getting sick or dying. The days were long and slow, children's games were so much fun, and people seemed to take forever to grow up – but it did not matter! With plentiful food and all the comforts they needed, people never ran out of excuses to celebrate. Their songs and laughter rang out across the big rivers and mountains.

In those times, humans and animals were still very good friends. Whenever the people of that country had a big feast, like a wedding, they made more food than any of the human guests could possibly eat, because the animals were also invited to come and share the food and drink. All the animals enjoyed going to such gatherings and looked forward to watching the singing and dancing. The dancing was always especially good. In one of the villages there lived a man who was said to be the best dancer in the whole country. At big celebrations, everyone looked forward to the moment when he would step into the circle and dance. Women ululated and clapped their hands even harder than usual. His family were all talented dancers too. Sometimes they would all perform together as a family – and indeed, those were always wonderful times. People had given this man a name, which expressed exactly the way he made them feel whenever he danced. That name was Mthokozisi – 'the one who makes others happy'.

Mthokozisi the Dancer loved travelling to faraway places to meet other people and learn new styles of dancing. Whenever he returned, he would rest for a day and on the following day, visitors would begin to stream into his house. They would have something to eat and drink, and then Mthokozisi would ask them if they wanted him to show them one or two of the new dances he had learnt. Of course they always said, 'Yes!'

Mthokozisi would stand up and sing a song, the drums would pound and he would start dancing. People loved to watch him dance and Mthokozisi loved performing his dances for them. He never got tired of sharing his adventures with others and relating his stories of the places and people he had met.

But it happened on one occasion that the travelling dancer returned from one of his journeys with a sharp pain in his chest. The pain was so severe that he cried and howled all night. The next morning the terrible pain was in his back as well. The day after that it was his feet which felt like they were on fire.

Mthokozisi's family had no idea what to do or how to help him. Since sickness was unheard of in those days, people had not yet discovered ways of curing illness. The poor dancer's agony was so unbearable that he ran down to the river to try and find relief in the cool water. His friends and family followed him, many of them jumping into the water with him, rubbing his feet, back and chest, trying to rub his pain away.

By that evening, every single person who had been in the river with Mthokozisi was as sick as the dancer. The next day all the women and children who had bathed there also fell ill. The wailing of the community could be heard from kilometres away. No one knew what to do. People tried to help each other's suffering by covering each other's bodies with leaves, in the hope that it would ease the burning pain they felt. They also used berries – anything at all. But it was no use. Several people died and many others became so weak that it didn't seem like they could survive much longer.

One afternoon, a wise Eagle Owl flew into the village. He had not slept for days because of the disturbance of the people's crying. He felt sad for their misery and came to see what the matter was. He was told everything. Eagle Owl flew away very fast. A short time later, he was back again with the news that Philani the Old Leopard was on his way. Philani was said to be the wisest creature on four legs. Many suspected that he had magic powers too. The suffering people waited, wondering how many of them would still be alive by the time the Old Leopard arrived.

But it didn't take long for him to reach them. Two large Gorillas had offered to carry the Old Leopard and run with him to save time. Soon he was at the village. Philani called everyone around him and told them to move slowly forward and approach him without pushing each other. He instructed that each sick person should touch one of his spots, wish for the sickness to leave him or her, and go back home to rest. Afraid though they were, the people controlled their fear and did as the Old Leopard said.

When the last person had touched a spot on the Old Leopard's fur and wished to become well again, they went quietly back to their homes as instructed. That night, Philani's voice was heard crying out louder than any living thing had ever cried. The Old Leopard's spots had taken over all the pain and illness of the people who had touched him.

The excruciating pain he felt from all those sick people was more than Philani could bear. With the rocks echoing behind him from his screams, the Old Leopard went back to his forest home and died there.

All the animals and birds mourned him, and so did the people of the village. They had so very nearly perished, and Philani had given his life to save them. Each of them was cured of the unknown sickness. They had no words to thank him, only tears of gratitude.

From that time on, people started looking for all kinds of medicines that would help to heal them from pain and sickness. Some of them became outstanding healers, and were given leopard skin to wear – in honour of Philani, the Old Leopard.

Cosi, cosi, iyaphela

HERE I REST MY STORY

LUNGILE

Illustrations by Kim Longhurst

LUNGILE WAS THE MOST beautiful girl in her village. People said it was not only the beauty in her face, but the beauty that shone from within that made her special. She had a very kind heart and took care to help her parents in whatever way she could. And she was always willing to help others in need as well.

The other girls loved to go with Lungile when she went swimming in the lake near her home. They played water games and had fun and laughed a lot. People joked that the girls went swimming with Lungile in the hope that if they stayed in the water with her long enough, some of her beauty would rub off on them!

Above all things, Lungile loved birds. She particularly enjoyed watching them fly, listening to their beautiful voices and admiring their colourful plumage. One day she and her friends were out in the forest together, collecting firewood, eating wild berries and having a good time teasing each other: 'Ooh! Your mouth is so purple – you look funny!'

'Ha! You can't talk, your tongue is practically black!'

Suddenly, the other girls realised that Lungile was no longer with them. They looked for her and found her in a clearing, standing by herself. Her arms were spread like wings and she was whistling sweet birdsongs, lost in a dream of her own.

The others teasingly asked her: 'What's wrong with you, Lungile – don't you like being the most beautiful girl in the land? Would you rather be a bird?'

Lungile laughed and said: 'Oh no, I have no wish to be anything except what I am! I love being a girl called Lungile. But I must admit that I admire the birds and their beauty. The miracle of flight and their marvellous songs fill my heart with joy.'

As Lungile grew older, she seemed to become even more beautiful. Many young men came to ask for her hand in marriage, bringing wonderful gifts for Lungile's parents. They were all so in love with Lungile.

The other girls watched enviously from their homes as, one after the other, the hopeful young men arrived at Lungile's door. The first man was very rich. The clothes he wore were of the finest material and even the way he walked showed how confident he was. He came with many expensive gifts, and the village women ululated as he and his companions entered Lungile's home. But when he left, his head was bowed and his shoulders drooped sadly. Lungile had said: 'No, not this one.'

The second man was extremely good-looking, so handsome that the other girls became weak at the knees when they saw him.

'This one is the perfect man for Lungile. His beauty matches her own,' they said.

But he, too, left with his head bowed and his shoulders drooping. Of him, too, Lungile had said: 'No, not this one.'

The third man who came was humble and kind. He promised he would always take care of Lungile and love her with all his heart, no matter what. Lungile's parents were sure he would be the one to win their daughter's heart. But when he left, his head was bowed and his shoulders drooped like the others before him. Lungile had once again said: 'No, not this one.'

And so, day in and day out, men were seen going into Lungile's home, full of hope when they arrived, sad and disappointed when they left. The other girls advised Lungile to stop being so choosy, or the men would get tired of asking for her hand in marriage. But Lungile did not seem bothered by this prospect.

One day Lungile's parents sat her down: '*Hlala phansi!*' ordered her father. 'Now, out of all these wonderful young men, do you mean to tell me that you have not seen even one that you like?'

'That's right, Baba. I am waiting for the man of my dreams. I saw him in a dream one night. He said he will send a bird to call me when he is ready to marry me,' replied Lungile, not daring to look at her father.

'Are you trying to tell me that you understand bird language too?' scolded her father.

'No, Baba. But I think I will just know when the right man comes along.'

Her parents did not know what to make of this. Her mother persuaded her husband to let their daughter wait a little while longer. But many people laughed at Lungile. They made up funny songs about her. They teased her that one day she would grow tired of waiting and be forced to marry a clumsy old bird, like a ground hornbill.

The other village girls got married one after the other, leaving Lungile behind. Her parents worried more and more as time passed. But Lungile stayed happily at home, working hard as usual. From old women she learned to make the most intricate beadwork, lovely baskets and grass mats. She also learnt many of the stories of her people.

Amazingly, her beauty seemed to increase even more. As time went by, she became so gloriously beautiful that even the birds seemed to stop to admire her. One old woman was heard to say: 'You know, this girl's beauty is not without its magic. Something special is still bound to happen for her – you mark my words!'

And so it happened that early one morning, a long-tailed black bird called Jobela came and sang for Lungile, just as her dream had promised. It sang a beautiful song: 'Lungile, hurry up, the man of your dreams is waiting for you at the lake!'

Lungile jumped out of bed and got dressed as fast as she could, repeating the words of the song to herself. She hurried down to the lake to meet her man – and was struck speechless when she saw him.

He was every bit as special as she had hoped he would be. There he was, surrounded by birds of all types and sizes. There were hundreds and hundreds of birds – small ones and big ones, water birds, veld birds and forest birds, perched in the trees and on the ground, hovering in the air or swimming in the water, gathered around this one man. When Lungile appeared, the birds all broke into song – the most beautiful chorus of sound you can ever imagine. Lungile's dream man ran towards her with wide open arms.

As they embraced, the hundreds of birds rose up into the sky in one big cloud of rainbow colour. Each of them dropped a feather, so that it seemed as if the whole sky was raining feathers. In the sparkling morning light, it was very magical to see those brilliant feathers drifting down all over Lungile and her special man. Old women and mothers came out of the village, ululating: '*Lilili, lilili,* what a wonderful day! Lungile is getting married – everybody come out and watch!'

So saying, they picked up the feathers and took them home to make the most beautiful wedding dress ever seen. Lungile's parents threw a huge wedding feast, filled with pride that their daughter had made such a good match. So that is how Lungile finally got married. She and her man loved each other a lot. They went back to his country and in their home, birds were always welcome. Their children knew that the birds were invited to play with them, share their food and teach them their beautiful songs.

Cosi, cosi, iyaphela

HERE I REST MY STORY

CROCODILE AND THE
MONKEY'S HEART

Illustrations by Kalle Becker

ONCE LONG, LONG AGO, a big community of Crocodiles lived beside a river and had a wonderful time raising their young and swimming happily all day with nothing and no one to fear. They ate anything and everything that looked inviting to them. Best of all, the food brought itself to them, so the Crocodiles never had to leave the water to find a meal.

Then, one day, the sad news came to the Crocodile community that the Crocodile King was very sick. Everyone was very concerned and went out of their way to try and help. All kinds of herbs and roots were found and brought to the King to eat and drink, but nothing worked. He got weaker and weaker.

An old grandmother Crocodile suggested that the heart of a Monkey be found. If the King ate the heart still hot from the Monkey's chest, she said, it would cure him. So the quest began.

Many respected hunter Crocodiles were asked to go out and look for a Monkey's heart. They all refused. They would not make fools of themselves, they said, trying to climb a tree to reach a Monkey. Monkeys were much too fast and clever – there was no hope of succeeding.

It was beginning to look as if the old Crocodile King would die. Then a young and ambitious Crocodile offered to help … or at least to try. The other Crocodiles laughed at him and told him to go and play with his friends.

'But I would like to try and help my King. Please give me a chance!' begged the young Crocodile.

'*Kulungile ke, hamba.* All right then, go!' said his father. And so the young Crocodile swam quietly up the river, looking for a tree that might be home to some Monkeys. Soon, he saw a big tree with long branches that flowed gracefully down to the water. The Crocodile gazed hopefully upwards. Sure enough, there was a young Monkey, curiously peering down at him from the tree.

'*Sawubona, Nkawu.* Greetings, Monkey. How are you?' said the Crocodile, smiling broadly and trying to sound friendly.

'*Yebo, sawubona* – I greet you too,' replied the Monkey cautiously.

'It's a lovely day today, isn't it?' said the Crocodile.

'If you say so. But what brings you here?' asked Monkey, still suspicious.

'Nothing really. I'm just admiring the way you swing from branch to branch with such ease. I really wish I could climb trees too – I think you are very clever!'

'Well, look at it this way, I can climb trees but I can't swim. You are very lucky to be able to swim so well. I think *you* are really clever!'

And so it was that the friendship started. Crocodile went back to visit the Monkey every day. They talked about all kinds of things that friends usually talk about, and this went on for several days. The Crocodile stayed in the water and the Monkey remained up in the tree … until one morning, when Crocodile arrived crying his eyes out.

'Everyone at home doesn't believe me when I say that you are my friend!' he sobbed.

'Why is that?' asked the young Monkey, puzzled.

'They say that I am lying. They want to know how I could be friends with someone so fast and clever.'

'Please stop crying like that. You shouldn't worry about what others say,' the Monkey told him, trying nervously to calm him down.

'Please come home with me. I want everyone to see us together, so they'll believe we really are friends,' begged Crocodile.

'And present myself as lunch to your friends and family? No thank you! Anyway, remember I can't swim, so how would I get to your home? If you want other Crocodiles to see us together then they will just have to come here to have a look at me.'

But the Crocodile cried and begged until the Monkey was persuaded to believe that his new friend would protect him with his life. As for the little problem of transport, that was easily solved. The Crocodile would carry the Monkey on his back.

And so the young Monkey, longing for some adventure, agreed to go home with the Crocodile. But he first asked the Crocodile to promise again that he would be safe and nothing bad would happen to him.

Of course, Crocodile promised. Then Monkey jumped onto the Crocodile's back and down the river they swam, gently moving this way and that way. It was a lovely experience for the Monkey. He was smiling nervously, holding his tail up in the air … and thinking how angry his mother would be to see him right now! But it was all so exciting that he did not want to go back.

They had gone quite a distance from the big tree that was Monkey's home when

Crocodile suddenly stopped and laughed out loud.

'How dumb you are indeed, Monkey my friend! The truth is, I don't like you at all – I just want your heart. Our King is very ill and he needs to eat the heart of a Monkey to get better. That is the only reason why I wasted my time trying to win your friendship!' said Crocodile, laughing some more.

Poor Monkey was terrified for his life. He knew he had to think very fast if he wanted to see his family ever again. Then he, too, started laughing. 'My friend Crocodile,' he said, 'why did you not say so in the first place? I would have gladly given you my heart! Of course we are friends and I care a lot about you and your poor King. But now we have a problem.'

'What problem?' demanded the Crocodile.

'You see, my heart is not in my chest right now. We Monkeys don't carry our hearts in our bodies. They are too heavy and would weigh us down as we moved from branch to branch. What a pity! If you had only asked for it sooner, I would have given you my heart the first day we met!'

'So where is your heart now?' growled the Crocodile.

'Up in the tree, of course. Let's go back and get it before your King dies,' said the Monkey.

They made a U-turn, swimming rapidly back to the tree. When they got there, the Crocodile commanded the Monkey to hurry up and get the heart. He felt angry with himself for wasting so much time befriending a stupid Monkey …

'I'll be back, just wait here,' called the Monkey. 'I will bring you my heart – and that of my brother as well. Ooh, I can't stand him! I won't be long.'

Monkey jumped up onto the first branch, and then the next and the next on his way up to his familiar home. Soon, he was standing safely on the tallest part of the tree. He looked down at the waiting Crocodile and laughed out loud.

'You are one stupid Crocodile! Where have you ever heard of anyone living without a heart in his or her body? My heart is right here in my chest where it belongs!'

This time Crocodile was crying real tears. He knew that now he would not be cheered and honoured as a hero by his community, but mocked by all the other Crocodiles and treated as a joke.

Cosi, cosi, iyaphela

HERE I REST MY STORY

NANANA BO SELE SELE

Illustrations by Junior Valentim

ONCE, A LONG TIME AGO, there lived a woman called Nanana bo Sele Sele. She was a hardworking woman with a happy, playful spirit, who had been widowed when her two children were very young.

Nanana's children were very, very beautiful and often people would stop at Nanana's house, see the small boy and girl playing outside and pause to admire them. Nanana and her children were very popular with all the people of their village.

But Nanana had just one little fault. She did not like taking advice from others and she could be very stubborn when she wanted to. For instance, she had built her house right in the middle of the animals' road.

Many people warned her that this was a very dangerous thing to do. They said that in such an unprotected place, so close to where the animals walked, anything could happen. They begged her, for her lovely children's sake, to choose another site for her house. But Nanana would not listen to anyone. She simply laughed and said: 'I am Nanana bo Sele Sele, who built her house in the middle of the animals' road because I fear no one!'

This was the response everyone got whenever they tried to talk to her about the problem. So, in the end, people gave up.

Nanana's children never seemed to be bothered by the talk of danger. They were used to seeing wild animals walking in front of their house in the middle of the road. Almost every day one animal or another would stop and ask them whose children they were.

Late one morning, a cousin of the children came to visit. She was a little older than Nanana's children. They loved their cousin very much and were overjoyed to see her.

Nanana looked at the children playing so happily together and she thought to herself: 'They are so content with each other that they won't even miss me. I'll just rush into the forest quickly and gather some firewood.'

So Nanana took her ropes and bush knife and, after saying goodbye to the children, hurried off into the big forest. She had been gone for maybe an hour when a Leopard with gentle eyes walked past the house on her way to the river for a drink. When she saw Nanana's two children, she stopped and asked: 'Whose lovely children are you? You are very, very beautiful!'

The cousin proudly answered: 'They are the children of Nanana bo Sele Sele, who built her house in the middle of the animals' road because she fears no one.'

The Leopard smiled and walked on.

Then a big Baboon came past and asked whose beautiful children they were. This time it was Nanana's children who answered: 'We are the children of Nanana bo Sele Sele, who built her house in the middle of the animals' road because she fears no one.'

By now, the children were getting tired of being interrupted in their game. They were hoping that their mother would be home soon. Just then another animal came by. This one was a very large Elephant with one enormous tusk. His ears were flared out and he was in an extremely bad mood! He stopped as the others had done and stared at the three children. They felt very unsafe.

'Whose children are you?' the bad-tempered Elephant demanded. 'And why are you playing in the middle of the animals' road?'

'We … we … we are the children of … of … Nanana bo Sele Sele, who built her house …'

'… in the middle of *my* road – doesn't she know that?' demanded the big, scary animal.

Before they could apologise or say anything more, the Elephant grabbed Nanana's beautiful children with his big trunk. One after the other, he lifted them into his huge mouth and swallowed them up. Their cousin screamed and ran into the house before the mean Elephant could catch her and swallow her up too.

Soon afterwards, Nanana returned with a bundle of firewood. She was surprised not to see or hear any sign of the playing children. Loudly she announced that she was back.

At the sound of her voice, the cousin ran out of the house, crying. She told Nanana the whole sad story of what had happened to her children. Nanana was furious. She wanted to know if the Elephant had swallowed the children whole.

'Yes, that's what he did. He swallowed them without any chewing,' the cousin said.

50

Nanana was very relieved to hear that. Telling the little cousin to dry her tears, she promised her that everything would be fine. Then, with her bush knife in her hand, she set off to find her children.

Nanana walked and walked into the great green forest. The first animal she met was the Leopard with the gentle eyes: 'Have you seen the one-tusked Elephant who has swallowed up my children?' Nanana asked her.

'You must walk and walk and walk until you get to the place where there is a clearing. No trees, but lots of white pebbles on the ground. That is where the Elephant with the one tusk lives,' the Leopard told her.

Nanana thanked her and walked on. Next, she met the big Baboon. He also told her to walk and walk until she came to the clearing with the white pebbles on the ground. Nanana thanked him too and walked on.

The further she went into the middle of the forest, the more animals she met. They had all heard that she was on her way to the home of the one-tusked Elephant to rescue her children, and they were eager to see what would happen. That nasty Elephant was a big problem in the forest. No one liked him, not even the other Elephants.

Finally Nanana arrived at the place she had been told about, a big clearing in the trees, where the ground was full of small white pebbles. She saw the one-tusked Elephant sitting lazily on his big bum with his huge stomach hanging out. The reason it was so huge was because of all the forest animals he had swallowed up.

Nanana stood angrily in front of him. 'Are you the Elephant who has eaten my beautiful children?' she demanded.

The Elephant hardly opened his eyes. He was so lazy and full that he could hardly even hold his head up: 'You must walk and walk and walk until you get to the place where there is a clearing. That is where the Elephant with the one tusk lives,' he told her sleepily.

'No, this is the place! And you are that Elephant! And I am not going anywhere else until you give me back my children!' shouted Nanana. 'Give them back to me right now. *Sheshise* – hurry up!'

The Elephant opened one eye.

Then he opened the other. 'Be quiet woman. Stop bothering me or I'll be forced to eat you up too!' he threatened.

'Go ahead. I'm not afraid of a mean, ugly, smelly thing like you!' Nanana replied.

And that's exactly what the Elephant did. He swallowed her too! As soon as Nanana was in the animal's stomach, she found her children. They were so glad to see her! It wasn't at all nice in that Elephant's stomach – dark and moist and it didn't smell so good. There were all kinds of other creatures in there as well, lots of little animals that the mean Elephant had eaten.

Nanana hugged her children close to her. Then she encouraged everyone inside the Elephant's stomach to jump up and down and kick and bang on the sides as hard as they could. The Elephant didn't like it at all! He rolled around like a huge, fat ball, groaning and holding his stomach and shouting: 'Stop it, stop it! Stop hurting me like that. All of you just get out.'

'How do you suggest we do that?' called Nanana bo Sele Sele from inside him.

'Any way you can. I don't care!' groaned the Elephant.

So Nanana took her bush knife and cut a little door on the side of the Elephant's stomach. And out came all the small animals, like the Hares, Meercats, Duiker and other little buck. They were followed by Nanana and her beautiful children.

Everybody was so happy to be out of there and thanked Nanana over and over again. Even the animals who hadn't been swallowed were grateful to her. That one-tusked Elephant was a horrible beast, a mean old bully, who was hated and feared by everyone.

That night, there was a huge celebration in the forest. Even the other Elephants came to join it, glad that the one-tusked Elephant had got what he deserved. None of them could understand how he had come to be so mean in the first place.

As for Nanana, she continued to live in the middle of the animals' road with her children. Many more animals came to see her and her children, who continued to grow lovelier by the day.

Cosi, cosi, iyaphela

HERE I REST MY STORY

ABOUT THE ARTISTS

Kalle Becker was born in Göettingen, Germany in 1964. He studied graphics, filmmaking, photography and Russian in both Germany and the Ukraine. As a filmmaker and actor, he has worked in Germany, Russia, Georgia and South Africa. He is also a freelance artist and has illustrated Gcina Mhlophe's story book, *Fudukazi's Magic*. Now Durban-based, Kalle is married to Gcina Mhlophe and they have one daughter.

Jeannie Kinsler trained and worked as a graphic designer for many years before she started to paint full time in 1998. She now works from home as a freelance artist and illustrator. Her favourite medium is oil painting and this is the third book that she has worked on with Gcina Mhlophe. Jeannie lives in Durban with her husband and three daughters.

Kim Longhurst studied graphic design at Natal Technikon, graduating in 1992. She lives in Durban and freelances as a designer, specialising in illustrations for the advertising industry. Kim combines a love of traditional craft techniques with computer-generated imagery. She recently won a Loerie Award in the Craft Category and has been chosen to exhibit for the prestigious Brett Kebble Art Award, 2003.

Lalelani Mbhele is a KwaMashu-based artist, whose formal art training began only after he left school. In 1997, he participated in a one-year workshop programme at the African Art Centre, and then went on to study at Natal Technikon for his Fine Art Diploma, which he hopes to complete in the near future. He is currently one of the resident artists at the Bat Centre Studio in Durban. His favourite mediums are woodcut and water colour.

Junior Valentim was born in Mozambique where he spent his childhood before moving to Durban. He did his diploma in graphic art at the Natal Technikon and has worked in the field ever since. A versatile designer and illustrator, Junior freelances for the advertising industry and a variety of publications. He also contributes social and political cartoons to the Independent Newspaper Group and is the creator of 'Grommet', in *The Independent on Saturday*.